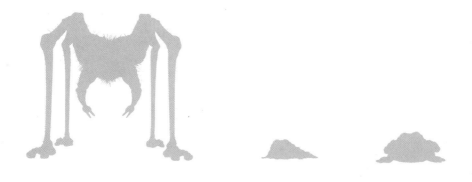

More Flanimals

by
Ricky Gervais

Illustrated by
Rob Steen

ff

First published in 2005
by Faber and Faber Limited
3 Queen Square London WC1N 3AU

Printed in Belgium by Proost

A CIP record for this book
is available from the British Library

ISBN 0–571–22886–0

2 4 6 8 10 9 7 5 3

Contents

There are a few more things you
need to know about Flanimals, then we
really should never talk of this again.

Chapter 1

The Flanimal Kingdom

How much do you know about Flanimals? How many Flanimals do you know? All of them? I don't think so. You're probably aware of the Frappled Humpdumbler but that's just one type of Humpdumbler – there's the Puggled Humpdumbler, the Squeebless Humpdumbler and the Flap-Toggled Humpdumbler to name just three. There are thirty.

Thirty Humpdumblers

Puggled Humpdumbler

Squeebless Humpdumbler

Flap-Toggled Humpdumbler

Sprot Tumbler

The Sprot Guzzlor is quite common and as you know loves to eat sprots, but what about the Sprot Tumbler, who just likes to roll them along the ground a bit? Or the Sprot Oggler, who likes to watch them? And of course, the rarer Sprot Mungler, who cunningly looks and acts like the Sprot Oggler so that the Sprot believes it is just being watched until at the last minute it is mungled senseless?

Sprot Oggler   ## Sprot Mungler

There are over twenty types of Underblenge, fifty types of Coddleflop and nearly one hundred types of Splunge. I don't think you need one hundred types of Splunge. You could get rid of most of them. Pointless. In fact, it annoys me a little bit. What about you?

Splunges

Anyway, there are so many types of Flanimal that we don't know exactly how many there are. There are more types of Flanimal that we don't know about than ones we do. How do we know that? We don't. Stupid, isn't it? No it isn't. Why not? I don't know. Do you? Ha! Not so clever now, are you? You will be when you've read this book. You'll know everything. That'll be good, won't it? No it won't, because there'll be nothing left to learn, and learning is great so that will be sad. So I'd stop reading this book now . . .
I thought I told you to stop reading. You've got a lot to learn. You'd better read on.

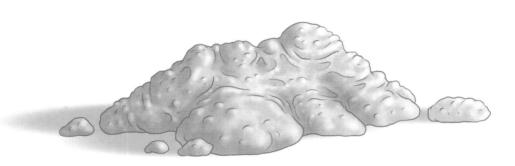

Globs of Gumption

Living Shnerb

Splungent Floob

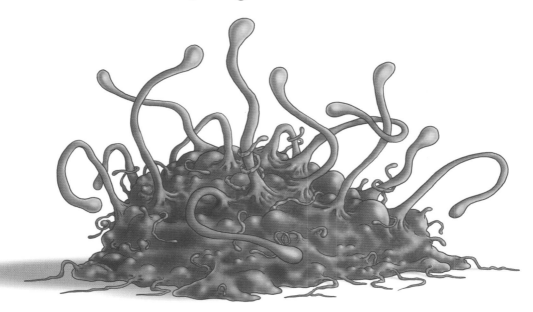

Where did all the Flanimals come from? Some people think they were made by a strange old man who lives in the sky. But not the clever scientists. They believe no one made them. They evolved. That means that over millions and millions of years Globs of Gumption and Living Shnerb gradually grew and changed into Splungent Floobs and Slunge Greeblers which multiplied and became the very Flanimals surviving today.

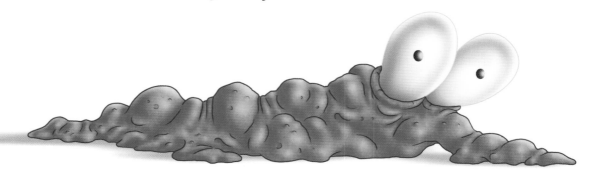

Slunge Greebler

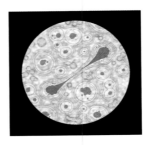

Splorn dividing as seen through a microscope magnified one hundred times

The very earliest form of Flanimal life was Splorn – really nothing more than a liquidiloid membrane, but it possessed the ability to reproduce itself. It could simply divide into two. It could do this because it had the building block of Flanimal life – a giant molecule called Dilopty Ribbidiloydo Nooflapid Happliassy Applyappalappalappalappa. Or DNA for short. Or DN for even shorter. D is about as short as you can go. Well, in any human language anyway. There is a sound that one Flanimal makes that is fifty times shorter than D. I'd say what it is but there's no point as you wouldn't be able to read it, it's so short. If I said it out loud to you, right near your ear, you wouldn't hear it. You'd need very small ears to hear such a tiny sound. Even if you wrote it with a big fat pen it would still fit on the end of a pin. That's how small it is.

Anyway, Splorn, millions of years ago, multiplied and changed in many different ways. It doesn't do it any more. Not sure why. I heard it was guilt.

DNA

Dilopty Ribbidiloydo
Nooflapid Happliassy
Applyappalappalappalappa

Chapter 2

Flanimal Evolution

Figure 1. Evolution of Splorn to Psquirms and Munge Fuddler

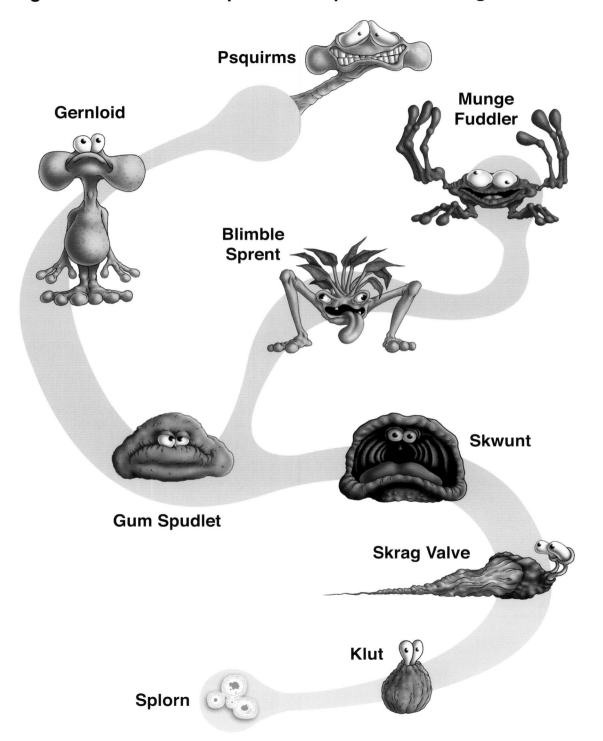

Figure 2. Evolution of Austrillo Ployb to Print and Edgor

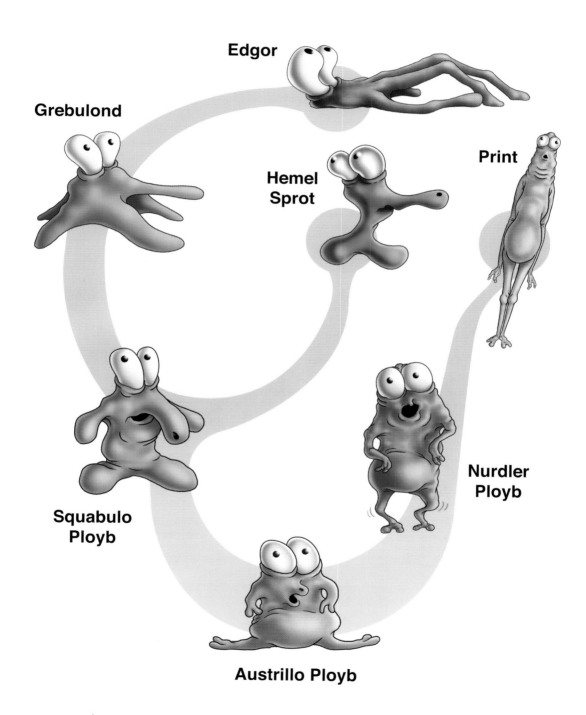

Figure 3. Evolution of Splorn to Squat and Dweezle Muzzbug

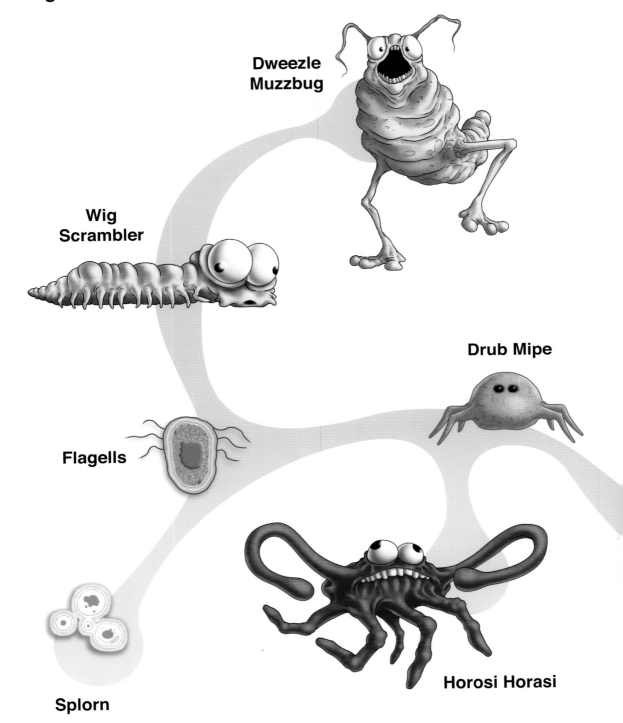

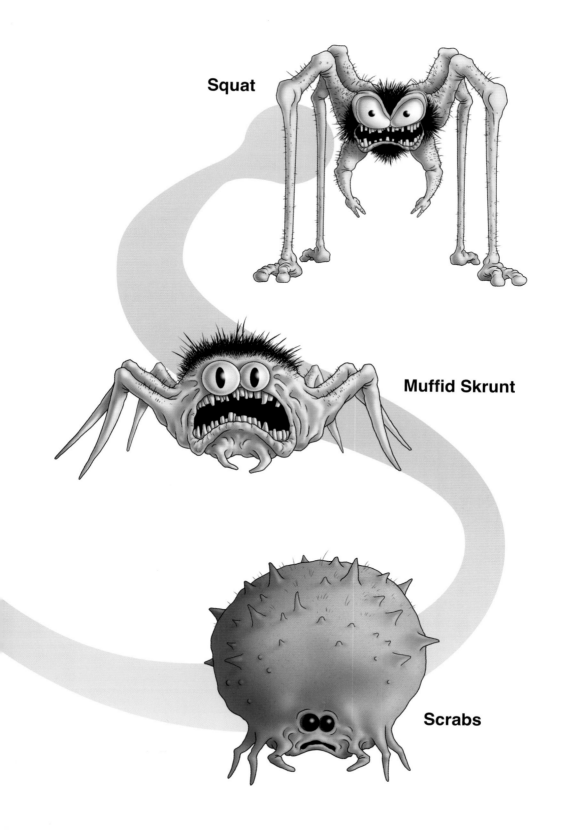

Squat

Muffid Skrunt

Scrabs

Figure 4. Evolution of Progulant Glob to Sprot Guzzlor

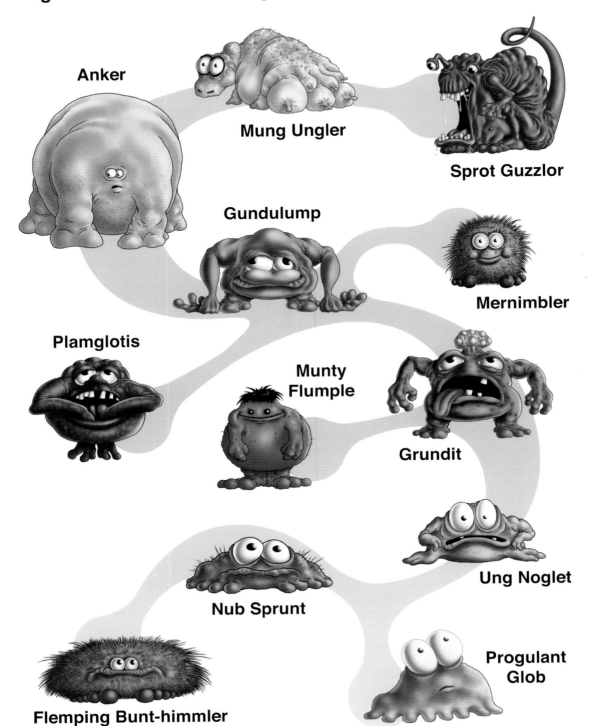

Fossil evidence shows there was a strain of Blunging that evolved millions of years ago but died out. It didn't die out because it wasn't as well equipped as modern-day Blungings – it was actually better equipped, faster, stronger, more intelligent and a prolific breeder. No one is sure why it disappeared, we think it just got bored.

This is what we think it may have looked like.

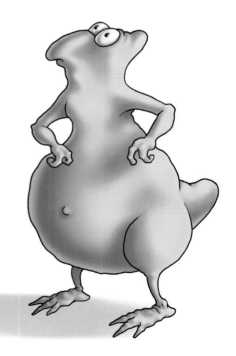

Plodonklopus

Figure 5. The Flanimal Family Tree

Chapter 3

Flanatomy

Flanatomy of the Glonk

Doesn't look like he's doing anything, does it?
Slice him open and see where it's all happening.

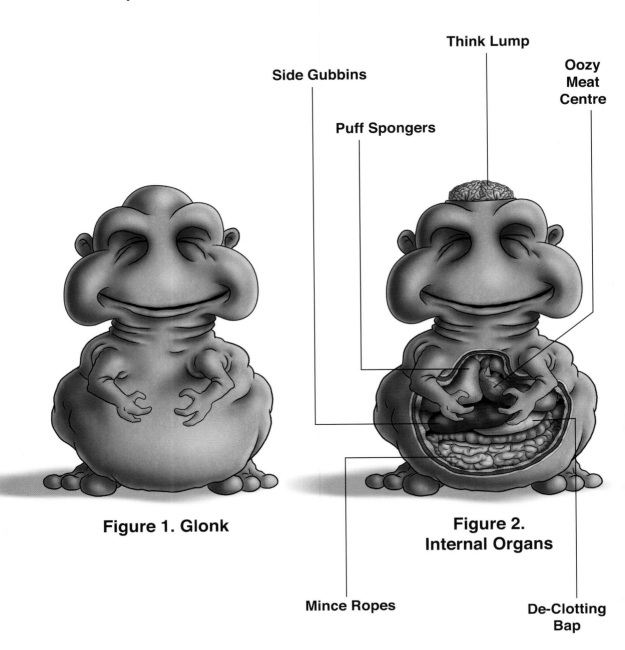

Figure 1. Glonk

Figure 2.
Internal Organs

Side Gubbins

Puff Spongers

Think Lump

Oozy
Meat
Centre

Mince Ropes

De-Clotting
Bap

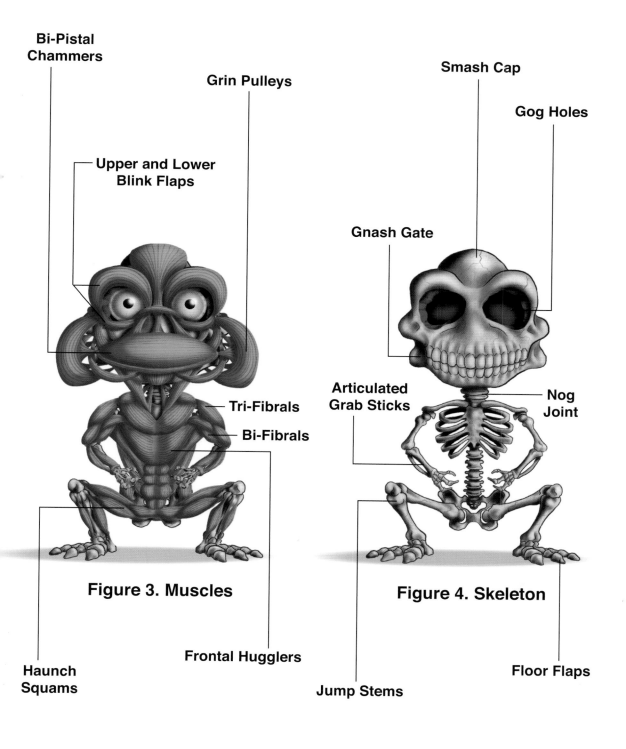

Bi-Pistal Chammers

Grin Pulleys

Upper and Lower Blink Flaps

Tri-Fibrals

Bi-Fibrals

Haunch Squams

Frontal Hugglers

Figure 3. Muscles

Smash Cap

Gog Holes

Gnash Gate

Articulated Grab Sticks

Nog Joint

Jump Stems

Floor Flaps

Figure 4. Skeleton

Remember this little fella?
Remember how cute he is?
Look at a skinned one.

Inside a baby Mernimbler

Chapter 4

Spotter's Guide

Skwunt

(Squintly Clamgullit)

Born with eyes inside its gapping nosh trap, this
cloppered valve sclap slams its mouth shut to stop other
Flanimals poking its eyes for a laugh. However, it is terrified
of the dark and opens up screaming, drawing Flanimals
from all around who poke its eyes for a laugh.

Plappavom
(Bilious Flob)

This bilgeulant flap of glunt has no mouth parts and so is unable to eat. It survives by gradually dissolving itself to provide energy for its bodily functions. Its only bodily function is looking around seeing what an utterly pointless and depressing existence it has. This means it lives quite a long time, making its life even worse. It gets smaller as it grows until it is just eyes. Eventually these dissolve too, and it is put out of its misery.

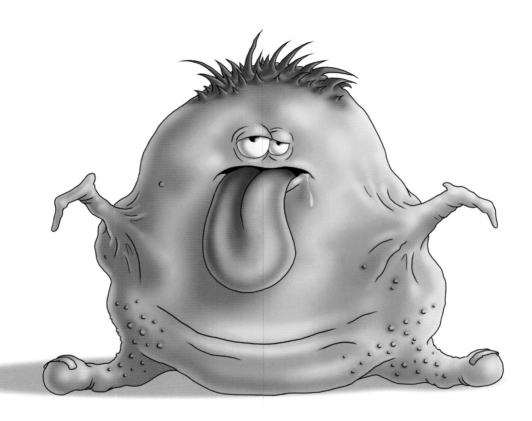

Fud Dumpton
(Mastrofud Poddler)

This romungular quock stumpling looks
like the most razbungled wumbligger ever.
It is actually quite serebental and aspireculous
in its feriping. Which proves you should
never go on appearances.

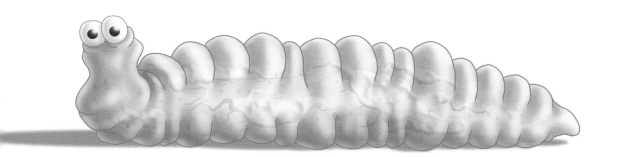

Grommomulunt

(Crumb Gullit)

This splunked-up spooge sock is the larval stage of the Munt Fly.
It has no mouth, ears, nose, legs or internal organs but just looks
forward to things changing when it sheds its skin and metamorphoses
into an adult. Unfortunately the only change that takes place when
it reaches adulthood is that its eyes fall off. It does shed its skin
but there is no new skin underneath so its insides just leak into
the ground. Have you ever heard a stain weep?

Horosi Horasi

(Razus Razus)

This scrabulatory skruntling is the fastest Flanimal on
the planet. When running over short distances it is able to
reach a top speed of fifty miles an hour. This is incredible
considering it is also one of the smallest Flanimals that exist.
It has been discovered that it is able to reach such speeds
because it possesses something that no other creature has –
legs that go absolutely mental.

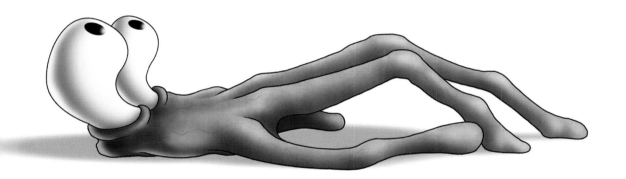

Edgor
(Carpus Ogg Grabbler)

This drudginous creepling is the slowest moving
Flanimal on the planet. Its top speed has been clocked at
nearly one mile a day. When moving at its slowest speed
it can actually move slower than some Flanimals
that don't move at all.

Dweezle Muzzbug
(Throxi Zub-Stumpling)

This scrammy beedle runs around wishing it could fly.
Angry, tired and fed up with using its legs to get around, it sheds
them so it can rest. Unfortunately legs falling off is one of the
most painful things ever and it screams itself to death in agony.
Hardly a rest, is it? So be careful what you wish for.

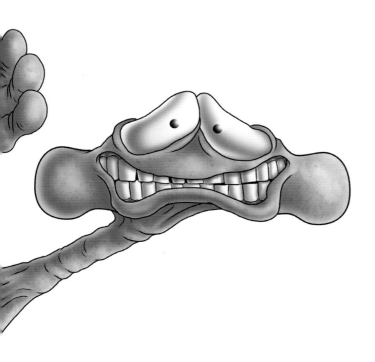

Verminal Psquirm
(Flungal Grindler)

The Verminal Psquirm spends its days poking its
head around or over things. Because of this we don't
know what its body is like. We can only assume from its
name that it is similar in shape to the Hordery Psquirm
but with superficial Verminal characteristics.

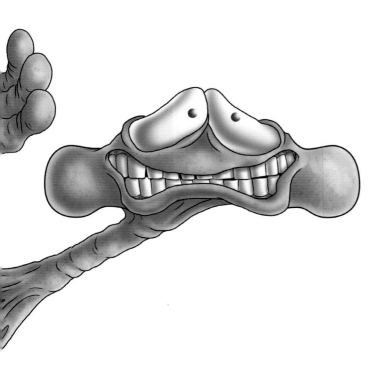

Hordery Psquirm

(Smarmal Grindler)

Very similar, aren't they?

By the way, the 'P' is not silent, it's pronounced *Psquirm.*
I said the 'P' is not silent, it's pronounced PSQUIRM.

Squat
(Psychus Crabantular)

This raknid scrabrapnor is the angriest maddest ripper-flan
in the universe. Whenever it meets another Flanimal it is so filled
with rage that it goes beserk with the gnashing and the smashing
and spiking and biting and it destroys it in seconds. This makes
it even angrier, because it can't carry on destroying, and the next
Flanimal it meets is destroyed even quicker with even more
gore clawing and dreadful head-shredding and aaghhh . . .
IT'S SO MENTAL!

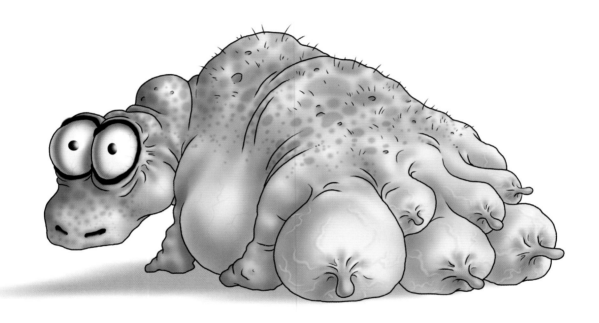

Mung Ungler
(Gruntloidian Mam-Langer)

This brontial mamb drudger is like a big sluggish liquid lunch. Flanimals from all around come and suckle on its rear milky puddings and there is nothing it can do about it. Inside it is screaming "roll on death."

Pong Flibber
(Flatulous Pumpton)

This pungent boggle-eyed guff bubble is quite useless.
Its only defence is to pump out its entire gaseous insides
at high speed to escape. The Flanimal it is trying to
escape from simply follows the smell to find the
creature de-ponged and flibbered.

Weezy Tong Nambler
(Fledge Sputer)

This flembulous frog-gossling is so utterly repulsive
in a pathetic, runtling way that it causes all other Flanimals
to instantly want to squash it for fun. Its defence is to flap
and lick. This is even more annoying and it therefore
gets squashed for fun anyway.

Prug Fuggell
(Bog Squabbler)

This drugulant testroprod is
nothing more than a simple Nad Snail.
And we all know what that means, don't we?

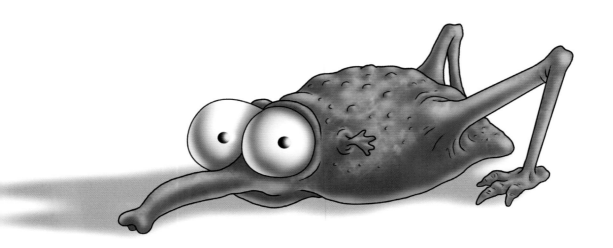

Gronglet
(Konk Shnerbler)

This tiny humfibiloid shnerbles along in ming puddles,
snorggling up micro-flugs, creatures so small they can't
be seen. It needs something bigger than this to live so it
starves to death within the first day of its life.

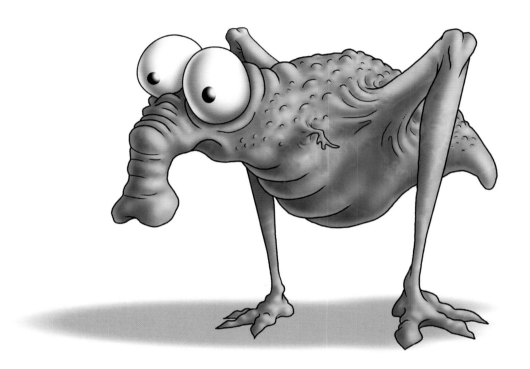

Spleg
(Konk Bwarker)

Related to the Gronglet but with greater snorggling
capabilities. It can snorggle up twice as many micro-flugs.
This means it doesn't die until the day after it is born.

Swog Monglet
(Mug Jizzling)

This huggly squibbling is a primitive pond slubber
that pulled itself out of the primordial sloob millions
of years ago. Once on land it was too fat and useless to
pull itself back in. Look at it. It is absolutely kippered.

Chapter 5

Flanimal Behaviour

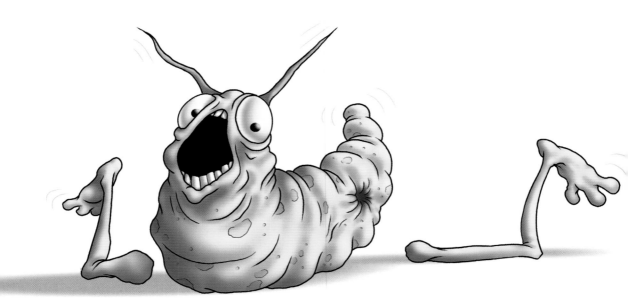

Dweezle Muzzgrub

**Dweezle Muzzbug after metamorphosis
from creepy-crawly into screamy death thing.**

Pong Flibber escape method

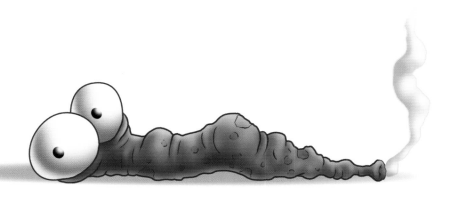

**Pong Flibber
De-ponged and flibbered**

Who's the Hardest?

As you've probably noticed, the life of any Flanimal is a constant struggle for survival. They have to live long enough to bring babies into the world to continue their species. With the threat from other Flanimals they have to sometimes fight to stay alive. Some love to fight, some are great fighters, but who is the greatest?

At 5 is the Blunging, at 4 is the Grundit, at 3 is the Sprot Guzzlor. We know the top two places are occupied by the Squat and the Adult Mernimbler, but because they've never met in battle we're not sure who would win. Who would you put your money on?

Adult Mernimbler

STATS
Weapons: Gore Horns, Clamp Fangs, Strangle Mits
Biting Power: 10
Strength: 10
Speed: 6
Aggression: 9

Squat

STATS
Weapons: Well clawed up. Two Stiletto Slice Sabres
which slash anything
Biting Power: 8
Strength: 7
Speed: 9
Aggression: More than 10, it tips over into mental

**Munge Fuddler trying to open
Offledermis for superior fuddlin'**

**Munge Fuddler and Offledermis
in an extreme case of over-fuddlin'**

Baby Grundit and Baby Puddloflaj

Just look how well they get on with each other.
They're so young and innocent they don't know any better.

**Adult Grundit showing the
young how to behave**

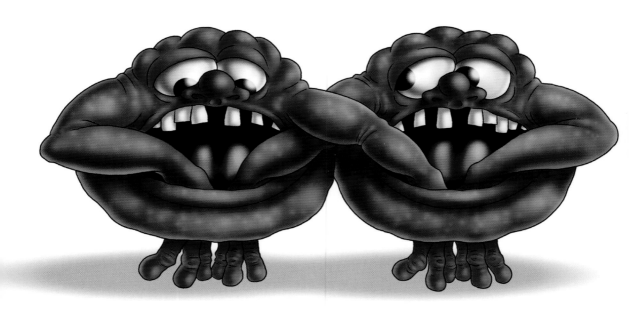

Twin Plamglotti

Born so close together they've
swallowed each other's arms by mistake.
Not a big problem, they're going to die anyway.

So now you know more Flanimals. Some of them are weird. Some of them are not so weird. But the weird thing is that the less weird ones are weirder than the weirder ones. Weird. But the weirdest thing of all happened exactly many years ago.

One day (two at the most) a baby Blunging asked his father a question.

"Father . . ." he said.

Obviously he didn't speak English. I'm translating so you can understand it. I couldn't even write what he actually said but the noise he made was like a mongoose with a cold. As the Blunging grows up it starts talking like a normal goose with a cold and laryngitis.

Anyway, "Father," he said, "what is beyond the Black Mountain at the end of the Dark Forest on the other side of the Sea of Night?"

"The what?" said the Father.

"The Black Mountain at the end of the Dark Forest on the other side of the Sea of Night."

The Father looked confused.

"Uh?"

"You know, the Sea of Night." He pointed. "Over there."

"Oh yeah," said the Father.

"Well, you know there's a big forest across there?"

"Yes . . ." said the Father.

"Well if you walk through that there's a big black mountain."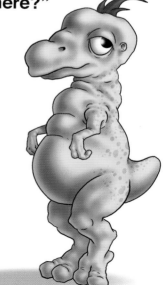

"Black mountain?"

The baby pointed again.

"That one!"

"Oh that one, yeah, sure. What was your question?"

"What's on the other side of it?"

"Other side of what?"

"The Black Mountain!" the baby said loudly in an annoyed way.

"Oh . . . nothing," said the Father.

"Nothing?"

The Father shook his head.

"You're not saying that to stop me going, are you?"

"No, there's nothing there," the Father insisted.

"It's just it sounds like the sort of thing a parent would say to stop a kid going."

"No, there's nothing there. Very boring."

"See, it's things like that. Why add 'very boring'? I didn't ask if it was a laugh there, I just asked what's there. It sounds like you're trying to put me off."

"No, there's nothing there."

The baby thought for a moment.

"Is it dangerous? Are there creatures so ferocious that I would be ripped limb from limb if I dared to venture there? And you just don't want me to be killed?"

"No, I don't want you to be bored."

"Right, I'm going."

"It'll take you a long time."

"Don't care. I can't wait to see what's there now."

"There's nothing there."

"We'll see."

"Nothing to see."

"I'm off. Bye."

So off he stritchly hopped. He passed an Underblenge sitting on a rock.

"Alright? Where you off to?" it asked.

"I'm going to see what's behind the Black Mountain at the edge of the Dark Forest across the Sea of Night."

"Oh yeah. I'd come with you but obviously I can't get off this rock."

"Shame," said the baby Blunging.

"Not really," said the Underblenge. "If I could get off the first thing I'd do is stick to your face and suffocate you to death."

They both laughed for ages.

"Anyway, must be off," said the baby Blunging. "Bye."

"Bye," said the Underblenge.

So on he went ever closer to his destination. As he approached the Sea of Night it started to get darker even though it was the middle of the day.

"Weird that, init," said a lonely Skwunt.

"You can talk," said the precocious young Blunging.

"Of course I can. It's about the only thing I can do. I'm literally all mouth," it said.

"No, I mean you're a fine one to say something's weird. You misunderstand me."

"Ooh . . . 'You misunderstand me,'" the Skwunt said mockingly. "I never said I was clever. There's not much room for brains when you haven't really got much of a head, you know. Anyway, where are you going?"

By the way, I should point out that Skwunts don't speak English either. They communicate with a noise that sounds exactly like an old sad monkey gargling.

"I'm trying to find out what's behind the Black Mountain."

"Can I come with you? Two heads are better than one."

"Not in this case," the baby Blunging replied. "Bye."

He crossed the Sea of Night and entered the Dark Forest, which was even darker than the Sea of Night. But then it was night by now so that's understandable. I know what you're thinking. How did a baby Blunging get across the sea when he can't swim? Well, he got a lift on a Frappled Humpdumbler obviously.

So he entered the forest. A forest full of creatures so hideous and terrifying to look at that they would cause anyone to die of fright instantly when they saw them. Luckily, as I said, it was dark so he couldn't really make them out. He went through the forest and there stood the Black Mountain.

"How am I gonna get over that?" he thought.

"You could always go around it," said a Gumbnumbly Knunk Knunk.

"What in the name of Grob are you?"

"Not sure. I'm not even sure if I am anything," it said.

"Well you've got to be something. I mean every . . . Hang on a minute. How did you know what I was thinking? I didn't say out loud about getting over the mountain, and yet you said 'You could always go around it.' How is that possible?"

"Walk," replied the Knunk Knunk.

"No, not how is it possible to get round it, how is it possible to know what I was thinking?"

"You were thinking very loudly."

The baby Blunging just looked at the creature.

"What a weirdo," he thought.

"Charming," said the offended Knunk Knunk. "Boy, you say what you think, don't you?"

"No I don't. That's the point I didn't say it. I just thought it."

"Loudly," said the Knunk Knunk.

"I'm off," said the Blunging. "Bye."

Finally, after six long days (and four nights), the baby Blunging had crossed a sea, passed through a forest and walked around a mountain. He had made it. As he stood at his destination, at the other side of the Black Mountain, he could not believe what he saw. A sight so devastating he could not speak. He could not move. He could hardly breathe. What do you think he saw? What do you think was beyond the Black Mountain at the end of the Dark Forest on the other side of the Sea of Night?

Guess.

Yes, that's right.

Nothing.

Flanimal Scale Chart

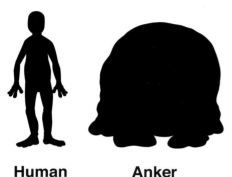

Human

Anker

Austrillo Ployb

Drub Mipe

Dweezle Muzzbug

Edgor

Fud Dumpton

Gernloid

Grebulond

Gronglet

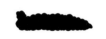

Grommomulunt

Gundulump

Horosi Horasi

Muffid Skrunt

Mung Ungler

Nub Sprunt

Nurdler Ployb

Plappavom

Pong Flibber

Progulant Glob

Prug Fuggell

Scrabs

Skwunt

Slunge Greebler

Spleg

Squabulo Ployb

Squat

Swog Monglet

Ung Noglet

?
size
unknown

Verminal Psquirm

Weezy Tong Nambler

So now you know more Flanimals.
In fact now you know about all Flanimals.
Well, the ones that live on the land that is.
I can't tell you about the Flanimals that live
in the sea because they are a bit weird.
Okay then, we'll talk about them next time.

Oh, I forgot to tell you about the Bletchling again.
What do you think it looks like?